STEEL FOR FREE

GALACTIC MERCENARIES

BOOK 2

OTHER BOOKS

Dragon Riders of Osnen

Trial by Sorcery
A Bond of Flame
The Warrior's Call
The Coin of Souls
Wing of Terror
Eyes of Stone
Tooth and Claw
The Servant of Souls
Smoke and Shadow
The Dark Rider
The Song of Bones
Sword and Crown
Tides of Darkness
Wrath and Ruin

Marked by the Dragon

Scale of the Dragon
Egg of the Dragon
Call of the Dragon
Wrath of the Dragon

The Fallen King Chronicles

Dragonsphere
The Fallen King
The Valiant King
The Restored King

STEEL FOR FREE

GALACTIC MERCENARIES

BOOK 2

RICHARD FIERCE

Dragonfire Press

e-Book ISBN: 978-1-947329-21-8

Print ISBN: 978-1-958354-25-4

First Edition: 2023

1

"WHAT THE HELL IS *that?*"

Jayde stood beside McCready at the observation deck window. The soldier had a look of confusion etched onto his normally stoic face, prompting Jayde to ask, "What's what?"

"That." McCready pointed. "That wasn't here before. It's been a few years since I passed through here with the Convocation, but that's new. Brand new."

Earth was the headquarters of the Convocation, the human government that spanned the universe. It was the beginning, the starting place for humanity. As technology progressed, humans colonized the rest of the universe. Jayde was excited to finally lay eyes on the planet. She had never been to Earth before, and this was her first time seeing how beautiful it was in real life. Granted, the holoscreens made it look amazing, but there was something about seeing it in person that couldn't be put into words.

Jayde took in everything, including the giant planetary shield that surrounded Earth. That was what McCready had pointed to. Hovering outside the shield was a massive space station covered in armaments like some sort of oversized intergalactic tank.

"It looks like they're prepared for war," Loch said from behind them.

"I was about to say the same thing," McCready replied. "It took us two weeks to get here, so it is possible the Thraan have already tried to attack human settlements."

"I hope that's not the case," Jayde said. "Either way, it doesn't look like we're going to be stepping foot on Earth without going through the Convocation, which is why we're here anyway." She glanced over her shoulder at Loch. He was sitting at the console piloting the ship. "You should be fine."

Loch shrugged. He'd agreed to come along, but he was worried that his warrants with the Convocation would get him arrested. Jayde had to give him credit. He'd spent years trying his damnedest to stay far from anywhere the Convocation had a presence. McCready had glimpsed Earth during his time with the military, and Klaus didn't seem to care much about Earth in general.

The sirens of the *Determination* began blaring. Jayde looked at Loch.

"What is it?" she asked.

"We're being targeted by the space station," he answered. "Our shields are up, but I doubt that's going to help if they fire all those weapons at us."

"Send them a communication. Let them know we're here to see whoever is in charge. Tell them we have a message from General Hans Otten."

Loch nodded and did as she asked. They waited for what felt like an eternity before the space station sent back a response. Loch tapped a button on the console and the screen above the window came to life. A man wearing a high-ranking badge of the Convocation appeared and Jayde tilted her head curiously. The man looked familiar for some reason.

"What's the message?" the man asked. He seemed side-tracked as if something more important was demanding his attention at the same time.

"We've got news from the edge of Apus," Jayde said. "General Hans—"

"Jayde?" the man interrupted her. "Jayde Thrin? Is that you?"

"Yes," Jayde said slowly, trying to figure out how he knew her name.

"The universe is smaller than you think," he laughed. "It's me, Logan Riggs."

"Logan!" Jayde shouted in recognition. "Wow, it's been a long time! You look like you've done well for yourself."

Logan waved a hand as if pushing her compliment away. "I'm just serving humanity," he said. "You said you have a message from Hans?

Where is he? He was supposed to report back weeks ago."

Jayde took a deep breath. "He's dead."

"What?" Logan leaned forward. "What happened? Never mind. Berth your ship and come aboard. I need to hear this face to face. I'll be waiting for you at the docking bay."

The screen feed faded and Jayde shrugged at McCready's questioning look.

"How do you know Logan?" the soldier asked.

"He was the pilot who rescued me from Ochillon. He was a new recruit to the Convocation back then. Do you know him?"

"I know *of* him. He made a name for himself in the Stargus Battles. His tactics against the Nerian fleet earned him a promotion to the big time."

"I'm sure he deserves it. I'd be dead if it wasn't for him. Loch, get us docked on the space station. Everyone's free to do whatever you'd like once we board. I'll let Logan know what happened on M44 and I'll find you guys when I'm done."

"Yes, Captain," Loch mock saluted her as she left the deck.

Logan Riggs. Jayde couldn't believe it. The man who had saved her life—twice—was here. Of all people in all the possible places. She remembered his handsome looks from when she was a young girl. He'd certainly grown more handsome as he'd aged. She'd felt silly about her feelings toward him when she was younger. She'd been thirteen and he'd been nineteen, but now that she was older, the age gap didn't seem so silly.

Jayde felt like a giddy teenager infatuated with a celebrity. Her stomach was doing flips and she had to reprimand herself. *Get a grip. I'm here for something serious and then I'm leaving. We've got to find our next job and put M44 behind us.*

She went to her personal quarters and changed into her armor but left her weapons. It was form fitting and she wanted to look good. The fewer problems they ran into with security, the better. Jayde ran her hands through her brown locks and checked her appearance in the mirror that hung above the sink, then left her room and went to the cargo bay. McCready was there as well, but he'd opted to stay in his regular clothes.

"You think we're going to run into trouble?" the soldier asked her.

"No, why?"

McCready smiled in reply. They waited in silence until Loch had docked the ship and confirmed it was safe to open the doors. Jayde tried to ignore the nervous feeling in her stomach as she stepped out of the *Determination* and into the space station.

Jayde's eyes widened and her mouth dropped open slightly in awe. The space station looked large and imposing from afar, but it was much bigger on the inside. There were people everywhere, almost all of them soldiers. Everything was an orderly hustle. Soldiers were hauling cases of what Jayde assumed were weapons, and dozens of warships were docked and being worked on by mechanics. It was mind-boggling.

"I'll see you shortly?" McCready asked.

"As soon as I'm done," Jayde confirmed.

The soldier smiled and disappeared into the crowd. Jayde walked slowly, overwhelmed by all of the sights and sounds. She was looking up at one of the vessels and almost ran into someone. It made her feel like a fool, so she uttered an apology and kept moving. Once she passed the ships, there was a long line of mech suits that caught her eye. They were single man design, used as weapons of war. Jayde was so busy admiring them that she didn't notice the figure standing beside her until he tapped her on the shoulder.

"You look enthralled by the mechs," Logan said with a chuckle.

"I was just thinking about how fun it would be to use one," Jayde said.

"Oh, they're fun, all right. And they can do a lot of damage, too."

Jayde turned to face Logan and they stared at one another in silence before Logan extended his arms to her for a hug. She stepped into his embrace and was immediately overcome with so many memories of her childhood. It seemed a foolish thing to think, but his hug felt like home. Logan released her and pushed her back at arm's length.

"I never thought I'd see you again," he said. "Ochillon was a disaster and when you slipped off the ship without telling anyone, I assumed the worst. I'm glad that I was wrong."

Warmth colored Jayde's cheeks red and she shrugged. "There were too many things that happened and I had to get out of there. It turned out to be for the best, though."

Logan nodded as she talked, that damnably handsome smile plastered across his face.

"I'd love to stand here and catch up on the last decade, but you said Hans was dead and that's a big problem. Follow me. It's too loud in here."

Jayde followed Logan out of the massive bay area and into the main portion of the ship. He talked about the space station as they walked, and she found the hallways and rooms of the vessel to be set up similar to those on her own ship. They reached a conference room and Logan held the door open for her. Jayde stepped inside and was greeted by a large rectangular table. The room was empty except for the two of them.

"Have a seat. Do you want anything to drink? Something to eat?"

"Food would be great," Jayde replied. "I haven't eaten since breakfast."

Logan sat at the head of the table. A computer screen was built into the table and he tapped a few buttons. The center of the table opened and a tray full of fruit rose from within. Jayde grabbed an apple and bit into it, closing her eyes for a moment in satisfaction.

"Wow, a real apple. You've done *really* well for yourself."

"We're stationed above Earth, so we have some perks," Logan said. He waited for her to finish chewing before he asked about Hans.

"What happened?" he asked.

"A lot. I don't even really know where to start. Hans died from being attacked by a Thraan. I think it was posing as a little girl, but she could have been infected."

"Infected? She was a dredge?"

"Yeah. No. Maybe?" Jayde shook her head. "I don't know. There was some really weird stuff going down on M44. We stopped there to refuel and took a job that ended up completely screwed. A diseased lyscren bit one of my guys and he turned into a sleeper. The entire outpost was overrun somehow. I don't think anyone survived. There was a girl that needed help, so I brought her onto my ship. After we left the planet, Hans's ship was there and he boarded us. Long story short, he took the girl with him but she killed him and his soldiers. He told me to warn the Convocation. Those were his last words."

Logan sat back in his chair and drummed his fingers on the surface of the desk. He had a concerned look on his face and he seemed to be having an internal debate with himself.

"You remember what happened on Ochillon?" he finally asked.

"How could I forget?"

"No, of course not. But I'm talking about *how* it happened. Those pods that were dropped from the sky?"

"I remember them," Jayde said.

"What I'm about to tell you is going to be hard to stomach. Those pods were filled with an experimental disease designed by the Thraan. They bombarded Ochillon with those pods as a way of testing it. It was an airborne version that they dropped that day, but they've since been changing it, perfecting it and making the disease stronger."

"So, the Thraan are behind the disease? What is the Convocation doing to combat it?"

"We're struggling to combat it," Logan answered. "Our scientists are working day and night to find a way to reverse it or at least cure someone infected before they turn into a dredge. It's not going well."

Jayde didn't know what to say. She'd known that something bigger was going on, but now that she knew it involved the Thraan and not the Convocation, it didn't make her any less angry. She took another bite of her apple and waited for Logan to continue talking.

"The Erillian's say they have a cure, but we haven't been able to confirm that yet."

"Why not?"

"We've been dealing with the current crisis," Logan said.

"What crisis?" Jayde asked.

"You haven't heard?" Logan seemed genuinely surprised. "We haven't been hiding the information. Hell, there's a giant shield around Earth. That should make it evident."

"Make what evident?" Jayde asked.

Logan sighed and looked down at the table.

"Earth was attacked. The entire planet has been infected."

2

"WHAT?" JAYDE ASKED INCREDULOUSLY. "What do you mean the entire planet is infected?"

"It's Ochillon all over again," Logan said. "On a much larger scale."

"What about the cure?" Jayde asked. "You said the Erillian's have a cure. Where is it?"

"Their Prime Minister says their homeworld has the cure. The Erillian's are one of our few allies, and they've been fighting beside us to fend off the Thraan. With the attack on Earth and the Thraan starting to invade the outer edge of our territories, we don't have enough manpower to send the Prime Minister to get the cure, if it even exists."

"Can't he take his ship there and bring the cure back?"

"His ship was destroyed in the attack," Logan said. "I'd offer him one of ours, but my superiors have told me that we can't spare any resources. Orders are orders."

Jayde leaned back in her chair and set the half-eaten apple on the desk. Food was the last thing on her mind now. It was her opinion that if there was a possible cure to the infection that the Convocation would spare the resources needed, but with the Thraan threatening to invade and kill off more

11

people, she could also understand their reasoning. It was a tough predicament to be in.

"How far is the Erillian homeworld from here?" Jayde asked.

"A couple of days using hyperdrive," Logan said. "Why?"

Jayde let his question hang in the air between them for a moment as she tried to harden her resolve. She'd need to talk to her crew, but she didn't think they would object once they learned what had happened to Earth.

"I'm a mercenary," she said. "My crew and I take on jobs to do all sorts of things. Delivering a Prime Minister and retrieving a cure for a disease is right up our alley."

Logan stared at her, amusement and … something else in his eyes. Or maybe she was imagining things.

"A mercenary, huh? It suits you. You've always been a fighter. But I won't be able to pay you. The Convocation frowns on hiring help. The whole independent image and whatnot."

"We'll do this one for free," Jayde said. "I owe you my life, and Earth is important. It's the least I can do."

"I'll let the Prime Minister know," Logan said. "In the meantime, would you like to get a drink with me?"

"I'd love to," Jayde replied.

Early the next morning, Jayde slipped out of Logan's bed and put her clothes on. Logan was asleep and she watched him for a moment before sneaking out of his quarters. She didn't want things to be weird when he woke up. Everything was set for her to take the Erillian Prime Minister to his homeworld, and now she just needed to confirm it with her crew.

The space station was massive, and she got turned around and lost several times before finding her way back to the docking bay. She boarded the *Determination* to find that everyone was back on the ship and had apparently been waiting on her.

"I wondered if you'd gotten lost," Loch remarked when she stepped onto the observation deck.

"Ironically enough, I actually did get lost," Jayde huffed. "Anyway, call McCready and Klaus up here. We've got a job if everyone is willing."

Once the entire crew was present, Jayde relayed the information Logan had given her. She didn't hold back any of the details, including the fact that they'd be doing this for free.

"I'm in," McCready said, almost before she finished speaking. "If there's a way to cure this thing, then it doesn't matter if we get paid or not."

Loch scratched at his chin and sighed. "Well, I can't say no after that mini-speech. I'm driving."

"Klaus?" Jayde asked.

The mechanic looked at her as if he hadn't been listening at all and shrugged. "I go where you go, Captain."

"Excellent. Thank you all for doing this. The Erillian Prime Minister will be here shortly. Unless anyone has an objection, I'm going to let him stay in Gavin's room."

None of them said anything, so Jayde dismissed everyone. Loch was the only one who stayed put. She sat down and tried not to think about Logan. He was handsome and had saved her life, sure, but he was a high-ranking member of the Convocation military. She knew he probably wouldn't settle down for years, not to mention he probably had women swooning over him constantly. She was just another woman in the sea of them that flocked around the man.

"What did you do?" Loch asked.

Jayde's attention snapped back to the present and she looked at the pilot quizzically. "What do you mean?"

"You're acting different," he said. "And your face is glowing. Wait … did you sleep with that guy?"

"Excuse me?" Jayde said, feeling defensive. "How dare you ask me something like that?"

"No disrespect," Loch said, lifting his hands placatingly. "I was just tossing out a guess."

"Whether I did or didn't is none of your business."

"Agreed," Loch said. He looked away from her, but she saw him grinning. Jayde rolled her eyes. She knew she shouldn't be so snappy, considering she always said things to him concerning his promiscuous lifestyle, but still. It wasn't something she wanted to discuss.

"I'm going to wait for the Prime Minister," Jayde said.

Loch did his usual mock salute and Jayde left the ship and stood in the docking bay. There were still people busy working, but it had lessened since her arrival. A few mechanics stood huddled around an Inquisitor ship, probably trying to figure out what was wrong with it. It reminded Jayde of her run-in with Lord Rasking. What would Logan say if he knew she was responsible for a Convocation lord's death? Would he arrest her? She didn't know the answer. She didn't have time to ponder it further anyway, for a tall hooded figure was coming toward her ship.

The figure stopped and looked down at her, then pulled its hood back. Jayde had never seen an Erillian before, and she was surprised by what she saw. The Prime Minister was almost seven feet in height. Aside from his face, he was hidden underneath long flowing robes. His skin was light green and his pupils were large black ovals. The white in human eyes was an ocean of blue in his. There wasn't a single hair on his head and Jayde wondered briefly if that was because he shaved it or because Erillian's didn't have hair.

"Jayde Thrin?" The voice was low and had a thick accent.

"Yes," Jayde answered. "Welcome to the *Determination,*" she said with a wave towards her ship. "It's my pleasure to take you to Erillia."

The alien tilted his head in a sign of thanks.

"Should I call you Prime Minister or …?"

"Yes. My given name is unpronounceable in the human tongue," he answered.

"Fair enough. Follow me, Prime Minister."

Jayde led the alien into the ship and took him to Gavin's old quarters. She had cleaned out the room on their trip to Earth and she'd stored his belongings in a storage closet. She didn't have the heart to throw the stuff away just yet.

"You'll be staying in here. Don't feel obligated to remain in here. You're welcome to go anywhere on the ship. Do you need anything before we leave? I noticed you didn't bring anything with you."

The Prime Minister peered into the room and seemed satisfied, though Jayde found it hard to read the alien's facial features.

"I have everything I need," he said.

"Well, if you change your mind, please let me know. I'll let you get settled and we'll be leaving in a few minutes."

Jayde left the Prime Minister and joined Loch back at the observation deck. She called Klaus on the intercom and confirmed the ship was ready.

"Do you have the coordinates to Erillia?" Jayde asked.

"Yes," Loch replied. "I updated our navigational maps from the *Titan's* archives. Either the Convocation has grown rapidly, or we haven't had a proper update in a while."

"Probably the second one," Jayde said. "Let's do this thing."

Loch's fingers were a blur of movement on the console screens and Jayde relaxed in the chair beside him. The *Determination* left the docking bay and headed into space. As soon as the ship was far enough away from the space station, Loch went overhead.

"Prepare for hyperdrive," he said. He waited a few seconds, then pressed a button on the screen.

Jayde stared ahead out of the observation deck window and watched the stars as they passed. They became like thin glowing strings stretched across the dark canvas of space as the *Determination* sped across the distance in hyperdrive.

"Next stop: Erillia," Loch said jokingly.

Jayde ignored him. Everything Logan had told her was troubling. Earth had been attacked. The Thraan were growing bold indeed if they had launched a strike on the stronghold of the

Convocation. The ramifications if Earth couldn't recover would be momentous. Humans had colonized hundreds of planets, but the heart of humanity was Earth. If it fell, what would happen? Surely the entire universe would suffer in some way.

"I'm sure everything will work out fine," Loch said from beside her. She looked at him and wondered if her emotions were that apparent on her face.

"I know," she replied. She had her doubts, but as Captain, she always wanted to put on a confident face. "What's our ETA?"

Loch tapped the screen. "If everything goes smoothly, four days."

"Nothing ever goes smoothly," Jayde muttered under her breath. If Loch heard her, he pretended not to.

The first two days went by with hardly any notice. The Prime Minister came out of his room only once the first day, and he kept to himself. Jayde noticed that he hadn't left his room the day before, and it was now halfway through day three and she had yet to see him still. She assumed Erillians needed food and water like any other race, so she began to get worried about him.

Jayde wandered around the ship, questioning herself if she should check on him. She wasn't familiar with Erillian customs and didn't want to offend him. After she'd paced her personal quarters so many times that she felt like she was going crazy, she decided to check on the alien and make sure everything was fine.

She paused outside the doorway and listened. There was no sound that she could hear, so she pressed her ear to the metal door and held her breath. Still, no sound reached her ears aside from the general hum of the ship. Jayde bit her lip as she raised her hand and knocked. *Please don't be asleep,* she thought. She stepped back from the door and waited.

Nothing.

Jayde frowned. If he was sleeping, she'd feel like a total jerk by waking him up. Still … some unnamed feeling was gnawing at her. She knocked again, louder this time. When he didn't answer, Jayde opened the door slightly ajar and glanced inside. No lights were on. It was pitch black and she couldn't see anything at all. Convinced he was sleeping and that she was crazy, she pushed the door open further to be sure.

The lights from the hall illuminated the first few feet of the room, but she still couldn't see the alien. Jayde pressed the button on the wall panel and the lights flickered on, slowly driving back the darkness. The bed was empty. Jayde stepped inside the room and her eyes were immediately drawn to the crumpled form of the Prime Minister. He was lying on the floor, his long skinny limbs sprawled out awkwardly.

She approached the alien cautiously and knelt beside him. He was on his side, and she gently grabbed onto his shoulder and rolled him onto his back. The alien's lifeless eyes were glazed over.

The Prime Minister was dead.

3

"HE'S LIGHTER THAN HE looks," McCready said gruffly as he hefted the alien's body from the floor and over his shoulder. The Prime Minister's head lolled awkwardly and Jayde couldn't help but grimace. "What are we doing with him?"

Jayde had been wondering the same thing. When they arrived at Erillia, what would they think when they found out their Prime Minister was dead? Would they think Jayde or her crew had murdered him? Since she wasn't officially hired by the Convocation, she wouldn't have their support if the Erillians imprisoned them.

She took a deep breath and tried to clear her mind. They could put him in a storage closet somewhere, but then his body would start to decay and the smell would be horrendous. McCready was staring at her expectantly.

"We could put him on ice," Klaus said. The mechanic had come up from the engine room to get something to eat and had heard her calling for help. He refused to touch a dead body, so Jayde had to get McCready involved. She'd considered jettisoning his body out of the ship but decided that the alien deserved a proper burial on his home planet.

"That's actually not a bad idea," Jayde said. "Thank you, Klaus."

"Just don't put him anywhere near the food, yeah?"

"We won't," Jayde confirmed.

"Speaking of food, I'm going to eat now."

Klaus left Jayde and McCready by themselves. Jayde rubbed her temples a few times and then motioned McCready to follow her. She knew just the place to put the dead alien, where he wouldn't contaminate any of their food. There was an extra freezer one level down that none of them ever used. They entered the elevator and went down to the second floor of the ship. It was the least used part of the *Determination,* but only because their crew was so small.

"We're about a day's worth of travel from Erillia. I'm worried they'll think we're responsible for the Prime Minister's death."

"Don't be," McCready said. "He doesn't have any wounds. I'm no doctor, but judging by the look on his face, I'd say he suffocated. It's hard to tell for sure, though. Maybe he had a heart attack or something."

"Do aliens have heart attacks?" Jayde asked.

McCready grunted in reply. They reached the spare freezer and Jayde had trouble opening the door. The seal had frozen and it required a little force on Jayde's part to break it free. A thick layer of ice covered the inside. Jayde moved out of the way and McCready laid the tall alien inside. The soldier was forced to tuck the Prime Minister's legs up in order to fit him inside. Jayde gently closed the door and heaved a sigh.

"I really hope this goes smoothly. I don't know what I'll do if we end up in another predicament like M44."

McCready tried to smile but ended up looking like a murderous lunatic. "If we end up in hell again, we'll get out. We always do."

The soldier had a good point. No matter the situations they found themselves in, they continually worked as a team and overcame adversity. Most of their problems stemmed from Loch's poor decisions, but still. They always worked as a team.

"You're right," Jayde said. "We've got this."

"That's the spirit," McCready replied. "Do you need me to do anything else?"

"No, thank you."

She stood there staring at the freezer door. McCready slowly headed for the elevator and looked at her from over his shoulder.

"You coming?" he asked.

"I'll be up shortly," Jayde said.

McCready shrugged and entered the elevator. Once she heard the door close, she sat on a crate and ran her fingers through her brown hair. She held up the ends in front of her and saw nothing but split ends. Her hair needed to be trimmed, but she didn't trust any of the men on her crew to cut it. They'd probably make it worse than it already was.

Jayde's thoughts strayed to Logan and she wondered if he was thinking about her as often and she thought of him.

"Probably not," she whispered aloud.

She stood up and started to head for the elevator when she heard a noise that sounded like it came from the freezer. Her face scrunched in confusion and she had a horrifying thought that the Prime Minister wasn't dead and they had just stuck him in a freezer. She hurried over to the machine and opened the door to peer inside.

The Prime Minister's leg had slid to the side and bumped against the door. Jayde was both relieved and disappointed that the alien was still dead. She pushed his leg back in and closed the door. His skin was cold and the chill clung to her fingertips. Jayde rubbed her hand against her leg for warmth and then went to the elevator. She came back to the top floor and went to her personal quarters.

She had told herself that she wouldn't message Logan until they had the cure in hand, but she couldn't contain herself any longer. Jayde sat at her desk and tapped the computer screen. It flickered to life and she recorded her voice only. It would arrive faster than sending a video file, and it allowed her to be free of her self-consciousness.

Once she finished her emotional tirade, she hesitated in sending it. She didn't want to come off as clingy, but she also didn't want Logan to assume that she had used him considering she'd left while he was asleep and didn't even say goodbye. She suffered a moment more of indecision and then sent the message.

"What's done is done," she whispered.

—

The next day, Jayde was awakened by Loch's voice over the intercom. She sat up and looked around, expecting to see him standing in her room.

"Jaaaaayde. Come to the observation deck, please. We're approaching the coordinates for Erillia."

Jayde rubbed the sleep from her eyes and rolled out of bed. She fumbled with her boots but managed to slip them on. The grogginess of sleep still clung to her but she remembered sending Logan a message the night before. *I'm an idiot,* she thought. She took her time getting to the observation deck and Loch was impatiently tapping his foot when she walked in.

"Look who decided to wake up," he said.

"Fight me," Jayde quipped. When she was tired, her entire demeanor was like that of a grouchy old woman. Loch must have recognized her mood because he stopped tapping his foot and didn't prod her any further.

"We're getting close," Loch announced from his chair. Jayde looked at him and offered a curt nod. He leaned forward and pressed the intercom button, then said, "Prepare for hyperdrive termination."

Jayde took a seat next to Loch. The sudden stop from traveling so quickly didn't impact anything inside the ship, but it did tend to make Jayde a little dizzy. Loch swore that she was lying when she said she could tell when the ship left hyperdrive, but she wasn't crazy. She could *feel* the difference.

Loch's hands were a blur of movement across the screens. The ship's speed decreased and Jayde watched as the starlight changed from stretched lines back to normal. It amazed her at how the hyperdrive worked. Before technology had advanced, she heard that it used to take days for people just to travel from Earth to Earth's moon. Now, any vessel could make that trip in a few hours.

All of her random thoughts disappeared as Erillia came into view. The planet's sun was hidden behind the massive world and everything was dark. It was much larger than Earth, perhaps three times its size. Loch whistled in awe.

"Request authorization to land," Jayde ordered.

Loch did so and they waited for a reply.

"Did it go through?" she asked.

"Yes, but something weird is happening. I'm picking up an encrypted communication. I think it's repeating over and over. Want me to try and decode it? It might take some time."

"Yeah. If we don't get a response, we may just land without permission. I'd rather have the go-ahead, but we didn't come all this way for nothing."

"On it," Loch replied.

Jayde walked to the window and stared at the planet. Her stomach churned with the same feeling she'd experienced right before she found the Prime Minister dead in his room. Something wasn't right.

"Loch, do a planetary scan for living organisms."

"Sure. What are you thinking?" he asked.

"It's what I'm feeling in my gut. I don't know why, but something tells me we're in for a surprise. How long before Erillia's sun comes around?"

"Can you give me one task at a time? You're killing me here."

"Sorry," Jayde said.

"The sun will be up in approximately five minutes. The scan will finish in six. I'm close to breaking the encryption on the repeating message. The *Titan's* archives are really coming in handy for this."

The minutes slipped by in silence with the exception of Loch's fingers tapping away at the screens on the console. Jayde watched the growing light of Erillia's sun as it slowly began to crest around the right side of the planet. It was blinding and she was forced to temporarily shield her eyes with one hand while the glass window darkened automatically.

Erillia was a planet unlike anything Jayde had seen before. Smoke and long lines of glowing red magma slithered along its surface. It seemed odd to her that a race of aliens like the Prime Minister would find a fiery sweltering world like Erillia to be livable.

"I didn't think Erillia would be such an ugly landscape," Jayde said.

"It's not," Loch replied. "At least, not according to the *Titan's* archives. It's a giant lush rainforest. Hot and humid, yes, but not fiery."

"Then explain what I'm seeing right now."

Loch was silent and Jayde glanced at him from over her shoulder. He was staring intently at the screen with his brows raised. He frowned and looked up to meet her gaze.

"This is what the archives show." The screen above the window lit up with a completely different view of the planet. There was greenery everywhere. Jayde compared the image with how Erillia currently looked and that dreadful feeling in her stomach increased. For a fleeting second, she considered the fact that Logan had sent them on a fool's errand. She immediately pushed the thought away. *He wouldn't do that.*

"Get closer," Jayde said. "How much longer on the scan?"

"Thirty seconds," he said.

The *Determination* closed the distance and it became apparent that either they were at the wrong planet or something terribly destructive had occurred on Erillia.

"Ten seconds," Loch said.

Erillia grew larger and larger as the ship got closer. Again, Jayde found herself awed by the sheer size of Erillia compared to every planet she'd been to.

"Scan's complete. It can't be right, though."

Jayde joined Loch at the console and looked at the screen. It *was* right. She knew without a doubt it was correct. The screen showed zero presence of life on Erillia.

"I'll run it again," Loch offered.

"No. It's not wrong, Loch. Erillia has been devastated by something powerful."

"The Thraan?"

Jayde suspected that Loch was correct. The Thraan were the only ones bold—or crazy enough—to outright attack the Erillians. They'd done it to Earth, so what would keep them from attacking Erillia?

"I would assume so. This is bad. If the cure has been destroyed, Earth is screwed."

"I've almost broken the encryption on the message. Maybe there's something in it that will give us some good news."

Jayde certainly hoped there was. She walked back over to the window. Erillia was a smoldering rock, nothing more. It was horrifying to think that the Thraan potentially wiped out an entire race, but maybe the Erillians were prepared for the attack and escaped.

"The message is decoded," Loch said.

"What's it say?"

"It says 'Flee, flee, flee. Flee to Hetania.'"

"What's Hetania?" Jayde asked.

"I'm looking it up now." He paused. "It's a moon near the planet Dreteron."

"So, there must be survivors there. Set a course for Dreteron's moon, then."

"Uhh …" Loch sounded nervous.

"What is it?"

"It's a Thraan outpost."

4

"WHY WOULD THE ERILLIANS be telling their people to flee to an enemy outpost?" Jayde asked. "That doesn't make any sense. It must be a trap to capture the survivors."

Loch shrugged. "It doesn't make sense, but what if it's not a trap?"

"How do you mean?"

"What if Dreteron's moon was the Erillian's safe place for a situation like this? If they didn't know that the Thraan set up shop there, the Erillians could have walked into trouble without knowing it."

Jayde found it to be a rare thing when Loch made a good point, but he was right. And if it wasn't a trap, then their alien allies could be in need of help. There wasn't much Jayde and her crew could do to assist, considering it was just four of them. Technically three, since Klaus wasn't really a mercenary so much as a mechanic. She turned around to face Loch.

"We can't go back to Earth empty-handed," Jayde said. "Not as long as there is a chance that a cure actually exists."

"Agreed," Loch said.

"How far is Dreteron from here?"

"Not far, actually. We can get there in a few hours. And the moon orbits close to the planet. I'll set the course if you want to speak with McCready about it?"

Jayde hesitated for a moment, then nodded. "Yes, take us to Hetania."

"Yes, Captain," Loch saluted. He began tapping buttons on the screen and Jayde left the observation deck and made her way to McCready's quarters. She doubted the soldier would take issue with the change in plans, but she liked to let her crew know everything she was privy to.

McCready's door was open and she peered inside. He was shirtless, which was normal for him when he was in his room. He had a bottle of vodka that he was drinking from and he was playing a game of chess on one of the holoscreens.

"Knock, knock," Jayde said.

The soldier glanced at her and nodded a welcome, then turned his attention back to the game. Jayde stepped inside and watched him play for a few minutes before clearing her throat.

"We might have a problem," she said.

"Yeah? What else is new?" McCready chuckled. "Problems seem to follow us wherever we go."

"Tell me about it," Jayde replied, rolling her eyes. "Do you want the bad news, the good news, or the possible bad news first?"

"Does it matter which is first?"

"Not really," Jayde laughed. "Erillia is a burnt husk. Loch and I think the Thraan attacked the planet. A scan shows there is zero life on the planet. The good news is that we decoded a message instructing any survivors to flee to Hetania, Dreteron's moon."

"I know the place," McCready said. "Spent a few weeks there with the Convocation."

"That could be really helpful, then. I'm not sure if the Erillians are being lured into a trap or not, because Dreteron is a Thraan outpost."

"Since when?" McCready asked.

"The *Titan's* archives on Dreteron were last updated just before we left. I'm guessing they parked an army on the planet and hit the Erillians shortly after. The planet is still smoldering."

"Bastards," the soldier swore. "I hope the Convocation can stop them before they kill everyone off." He took a swig from his bottle. "So, what's our plan?"

"Ideally, we'll land on the moon without being seen by the Thraan and find the Erillians. Get the cure and high-tail it back to Earth."

"Sounds simple enough," McCready said. "We never do things the simple way, though."

"I know. Be ready to go in guns blazing. It's probably going to get ugly quick."

"I'll be ready," McCready said. He took another drink from his bottle and moved a piece on the chess board, beating the computer.

Jayde left the soldier and went to her personal quarters to change into her armor. They could very well be walking into a trap, but the chances of getting the cure far outweighed the danger in her opinion. It was a literal life and death scenario back on Earth without it.

By the time Jayde had changed, eaten something, taken a quick nap and made her way back to the observation deck, Hetania was in view. The moon had an orange glow around its gray surface. The planet Dreteron loomed behind the moon, dark and ominous.

"Too bad we don't have any way to cloak our presence," Loch complained. "If the Thraan see us, we're toast."

Jayde had been meaning to have cloaking technology installed on the *Determination,* but she'd been putting it off due to money constraints. She decided to get it done once they were done rescuing Earth.

"I've located the source of the signal," Loch said.

"Set us down somewhere nearby," Jayde instructed. "I don't want to land in the middle of a trap."

"Will do. I think I might be right about this not being a trap. The signal is coming through strong, but when I scan the coordinates of the source, there's nothing there. I think the Erillians are hiding with some sort of shroud."

"I hope that's the case," Jayde said.

She stood at the window as they approached the moon and watched for any sign of Thraan ships. Even though she didn't see anything, that didn't mean they hadn't already picked up the *Determination* on their radar.

Loch landed the ship roughly half a mile from the coordinates of the source. He'd also scanned the atmosphere and confirmed there was no oxygen, so they were forced to wear full-body suits over their armor. The material was lightweight, but the headgear was cumbersome. Jayde hated when they encountered places without oxygen. It complicated things.

Jayde, Loch, and McCready departed the vessel, leaving Klaus behind to watch the ship. The moon had gravity, so they were able to walk normally. The terrain was rocky and mostly flat, but a few rolling hills broke up the monotony. The rocks and the dirt were gray colors, reminding Jayde of a shale pit she'd once seen. Loch led the way, holding up a portable holoscreen and shouting into his suit's microphone every few minutes with how much further they had to go.

It took them the better part of an hour to reach the coordinates of the signal. Loch warned them once they were within three hundred feet and they all drew their guns and slowed their pace. As they closed the distance, Jayde spotted a camp. It stood in stark contrast to the gray landscape around it, but Jayde knew Loch's assessment of a shroud hiding its location must be accurate.

"I'll take point," McCready's voice crackled in Jayde's headset.

"I'll bring up the rear," Jayde replied.

She watched the soldier crouch down and jog closer to the camp's border. There were no signs of movement, but Jayde knew better than to let her guard down. She held back and waited until McCready disappeared into the camp. Small temporary buildings dotted the area. Some were teal and others were purple, their vibrant colors shimmering in the light.

Loch was kneeling beside one of the buildings, peering through the scope on his rifle. Jayde looked around for McCready, but she'd lost sight of the soldier.

"Anything?" she asked.

"Not that I can see," Loch replied.

"McCready?"

He didn't answer. Jayde frowned and waited a moment longer before repeating his name. There was still no response.

"Can you see McCready, Loch?"

She watched the pilot slowly move around the building until he was no longer visible. Jayde waited impatiently and was about to start walking closer to the camp when she saw Loch reappear.

"I don't see him, but I saw something on the other side of the camp. It was tall, just like the Prime Minister. It could have been an Erillian."

Hope burned in her chest. They had found the Erillians, and hopefully, the cure.

"I'm coming to your position. Keep your eyes peeled."

Jayde tried to mimic McCready's crouch and hurried over to the building where Loch was. She reached his side and paused to catch her breath. Sweat was running down her forehead and her back.

"These damn suits are like an oven," she grumbled.

"Tell me about it," Loch said. "At least you don't have sweat running down your balls."

She ignored his comment and went around the other side of the building. There were more of the odd colored buildings, as well as large square items that looked like crates of supplies. The more she saw, the more Jayde was convinced that this was the Erillian camp and not some trap set by the Thraan.

Jayde stood up and started to walk further into the camp when McCready's voice came through the suit speakers.

"Stay where you are. There's a group hiding behind the building ahead of you and they don't look friendly."

"Where you are?" Jayde asked.

"Look up and to your left."

Jayde did so and saw the soldier's head peeking over the top of one of the buildings. If he hadn't told her where he was, she would never have found him.

"Do you see anyone else?" she asked.

"No, but I'm sure there are more around here somewhere. This camp is too large for there not to be."

"We need to speak with the Erillians," Jayde said. "We can't play hide and seek forever."

McCready was silent for a moment, then he said, "I know. Move out into the open slowly. If I see anything that looks like danger, I'm firing."

"Fair enough."

Jayde walked away from the building slowly, her gun lowered. She didn't want to appear threatening. Her heart was pounding in her chest, but she kept her breathing even. A drop of sweat rolled into her eye and she blinked rapidly to clear it away, which only made it worse. She paused and held the eye shut, hoping that would help.

"What's wrong?" McCready asked.

"Nothing, I'm just sweating into my eyes. I can't see—"

Her words were cut off as a group of Erillians came storming out from behind the building ahead of her. They were tall like the Prime Minister, but they looked nothing like him. Their flesh was a darker shade of green and they had wicked looking yellowed spikes down the front of their arms. Jayde dropped her gun on the ground and held her arms up.

"I'm Jayde Thrin of the *Determination*," she called out, using her suit's external speakers. "I'm here on behalf of the Convocation. I was told you have a cure for the disease that the Thraan have attacked Earth with."

One of the Erillians stepped forward, his gun still trained on her. He looked reptilian and his facial features unreadable. He cocked his head from one side to the other, then chirped a command to his fellows. They lowered their weapons. Jayde stood still, not sure if it was safe to lower her arms.

"Tell me, Jayde Thrin of the *Determination,* why did the Convocation ignore our plea for assistance against the Thraan?"

Jayde felt her heart fall into her stomach. Logan didn't mention anything about that to her. She swallowed hard.

"I don't know," she said. "I'm not part of the Convocation, I'm just here on behalf of them, on behalf of Earth. If I had to guess, I'd say they are busy defending against the Thraan themselves. I'm here because the Convocation couldn't spare any resources to investigate the cure themselves."

The Erillians nostrils flared open momentarily. It took another step closer to Jayde and sniffed the air. Jayde suddenly realized the Erillian wasn't male but female. The armor covering its torso did well to hide the Erillian's breasts.

"You're telling the truth," the alien said, a statement and not a question. It lowered the weapon and Jayde lowered her arms. She was thankful for that, too. Her arms were beginning to shake from the exertion.

"Tell your man to come down from his perch."

"McCready," Jayde said. "You can come down here. They know you're up there."

She received a grunt in reply. Loch joined them, escorted by two Erillians.

"Are you the leader here?" Jayde asked the female Erillian.

"Yes."

"Do you really have the cure to the Thraan disease?"

"Yes."

Jayde breathed a sigh of relief. "That's great news. Can we have it?"

"No," the Erillian replied.

5

"No? Why not? We need it or the entire population of Earth will be dead!"

"Do the people on your planet give things away for free?" The Erillian's head snaked to the right.

"Sometimes," Jayde replied.

"Valuable things?" the alien clarified.

"Not so much," Jayde admitted.

"Then you will understand my position. I have something you need, and we are also in need of something."

"Sure. What is it?"

The Erillian pointed toward the planet Dreteron. "We need a part for our vessel. The Thraan have what we need, but we cannot get it from them. If you can retrieve the part, we will give you the cure."

"How do we get the part?" Jayde asked. "The Thraan will kill us if they see us."

"You understand our dilemma, for we are in the same position. We cannot leave this place without the part we need, but the Thraan will finish their extermination of my people if they find us."

Jayde bit her lower lip in thought. The Thraan were vicious, barbaric creatures. If her crew was caught, not only would the cure not reach Earth, but there was no telling what the aliens would do to her and her crew before killing them. Yet Jayde knew that the hope of humanity rested on her shoulders. She looked from Dreteron to the Erillian.

"How do we get onto the planet without being seen?"

The Erillian's eyes blinked and Jayde thought she saw two different membranes on each eye. The alien leader stepped closer and Jayde had to tilt her head back to continue to meet the Erillian's gaze.

"Some distance from here there is a cave. The Thraan are using the cave to harvest crystals for fuel from the moon's core. At the cave, there is a transport tunnel that leads to Dreteron. I have never been inside it, but I have seen it work. It will take you to the planet, and it will be safer than flying your ship there."

"Any other wisdom you want to share?" Jayde asked. "What's the easiest way to kill a Thraan?"

The Erillian made a howling noise that sounded like a dog. It took Jayde a moment to realize the Erillian was laughing.

"Silly human, you don't kill the Thraan." The alien grew somber, the laughter abruptly coming to an end. "You run from the Thraan."

The ominous tone of the Erillian sent a shudder up Jayde's spine. She gritted her teeth and forced the uneasy feeling away. She was a mercenary, a fighter. She had killed plenty, both humans and aliens. Granted, she'd never seen a Thraan before, but what did that matter? Besides, she had McCready and Loch with her. Together, they were an unstoppable team. The events on M44 proved that.

"Fair enough. What does this part look like? Where can we find it?"

The Erillian produced a holoscreen from her waist and tapped a button. An image of a small square shaped item appeared. It looked similar to a memory chip.

"This is what we need," the alien said. "It powers our engines."

Judging by the size of the thing, Jayde didn't think it would power a child's toy. She shrugged and had Loch copy the image to his holoscreen in case they had trouble recognizing it later.

"Once we get to Dreteron, where do we find this part?"

"Our spies have told us that the Thraan have built a city on the planet. Within that city, there is a market that has everything we need. The Thraan's ships are similar to our own, but this part is very valuable. It will be secured. You will need to find a way through the security." The Erillian paused and Jayde thought she could see sadness in the alien's eyes.

"Remember that you are only seeking the part for our ship. Do not let anything you see make you forget why you are there."

"Don't worry about us," Jayde said. "This isn't our first job."

"We will wait here for you. If you do not return in two days, I will assume you have been killed."

"There's a phrase we have where I come from," Jayde said. "You know what assuming does?"

The Erillian tilted its head curiously. "What?"

Jayde laughed. "I'll tell you when I bring the part back."

"I have something that will be of use to you." The leader turned to one of her soldiers and made a chirping sound. The soldier disappeared inside the building nearby and returned with a handful of devices. He handed them to Jayde and she passed one to Loch and one to McCready.

"What are they?" Jayde asked.

"They will make you invisible for a short period of time. Once their power source has been used, they will recharge themselves but it will take some time. Use them wisely."

"Thank you," Jayde said, admiring the technology. She turned to Loch and McCready. "Let's make this one quick, yeah?"

—

The transport tunnel was unlike anything Jayde had seen before. It looked like a long elevator shaft that had been turned sideways and stretched from the moon to the planet Dreteron. It was a wonder of technology, and Jayde couldn't help but wonder how in the universe the Thraan had built it.

"Ever seen one of those?" she asked McCready with a nod at the tunnel.

"I've seen a lot of things in my time, but nothing that impressive. If the Convocation has the same technology, they've kept it well hidden."

The three of them were hiding behind a wall of metal shipping crates, waiting until they were sure that no one was around. After about ten minutes, Jayde walked out into the open cautiously, her rifle at the ready. The place was silent.

"It's clear," she called out.

Loch and McCready joined her and they walked toward the tunnel. The entrance was suspended off the ground and a makeshift set of stairs had been built out of large rocks. The tunnel was transparent and undulated back and forth like some sort of giant serpent.

"That thing doesn't look very safe. Or study," Loch said.

"Well, unless you want to fly right into Death's waiting arms, it's our only option."

Jayde put on her best show of confidence, but she was thinking the same thing as Loch. The swaying passageway didn't look safe. She inhaled deeply and strode to the opening, pausing at the entrance. If they ran into Thraan soldiers on the way across, there would be nowhere to go. They would be forced to fight.

You run from the Thraan. The Erillian's words rang in Jayde's mind. She pushed her hesitations aside and stepped across the threshold. She wasn't sure what to expect, but standing in the tunnel was no different than standing on the ground of the moon. There was a stronger gravity, like that on the *Determination.*

"Lead the way," Loch said.

The planet looked like it was a thousand miles away, but they didn't have any other option. Jayde led them across the bridge. She guessed there was some sort of wormhole tech being used, because it seemed like they traveled about a mile by her best estimate, and they reached the end within an hour. The gravity was not as strong as they got further inside the tunnel and it made traveling its length slow and arduous. The tunnel's exit was the same as its entrance, suspended above the ground. There were actual stairs on this end, and Jayde did a quick scan of the area before stepping down.

There were no guards present, for which Jayde was thankful. McCready came out next and Loch was last. They stood at the foot of the stairs, guns ready, but there was no sign of any living creature.

"Look," Loch pointed ahead.

The lights of the Thraan city illuminated the landscape in a ghostly sheen. There were muffled sounds and Jayde looked at McCready curiously.

"Does Dreteron have oxygen?" she asked.

"I'm not sure," the soldier answered. "Check the holoscreen," he told Loch.

Loch pulled the device up and typed onto the small screen. He smiled and opened his suit helmet to Jayde's horrified facial expression. He took a deep breath.

"Thank God!" he laughed. "I was burning up in this suit."

"You didn't even test the atmosphere!" she berated him. "Oxygen or not, you could have just died!"

"I was feeling confident," Loch said sheepishly.

Jayde shook her head in aggravation and removed her own helmet. The cool air on her face felt amazing.

"All right, take the suits off. We'll have to hide them somewhere until we come back through here. It'll definitely make sneaking into the city easier without these things."

McCready found a shallow hole next to a crate and they tossed their suits inside, then moved the crate over the hole. With that task completed, they closed the distance to the city and waited near a wall while Loch relieved himself. He rejoined them a few moments later with a frown on his face.

"What's wrong?" Jayde asked.

"I don't like not being able to wash my hands," he complained.

"Did you piss on them?" McCready asked.

"No," Loch replied indignantly.

"There are only two reasons why a man washes his hands after pissing," the soldier said. "Either you pissed on your hands, or your hose is dirty."

"Seriously?" Jayde growled. "We don't have time for this nonsense. We've got to figure out how to get into the market without being seen. Any ideas?"

McCready scratched his chin thoughtfully and then grunted. "No."

Loch shrugged, but then squinted past Jayde. "I think I have an idea," he said.

Jayde turned around and saw what Loch was looking at. Her blood boiled at the sight. A small crowd of humans was huddled in a metal cage next to a plain building. Their clothing was a myriad of patches of all different materials and they looked starved. There was one human dressed in nice attire standing near the cage door.

"What is this?" Jayde demanded. "What's going on here? They look like slaves."

"They are slaves," McCready confirmed. "The Thraan take captives and force them to do anything and everything for them. This is what the Erillian meant when she said to remember why we're here."

"We can't leave them here," Jayde said. "They need our help."

"I don't disagree, but most of them have probably been slaves their entire lives. They don't even know the concept of freedom. You know I'll back you behind whatever you want to do, but I think getting the cure back to Earth is the top priority right now."

Jayde knew McCready was right. They didn't have enough time or resources to do everything. She stared at the people, caged up like wild animals. Some of them had a feral look in their eyes, as though all of their humanity had been forgotten. And the human guard didn't seem to have any problem with their predicament. She guessed he was brainwashed into serving the Thraan.

"Damn it," she cursed, kicking at the ground. "Let's find the part we need before I change my mind and mount a rebellion here and now."

"The part is supposed to be in the marketplace," Loch said. "I was thinking if we pretend to be slaves, we could possibly get into the marketplace and find it. We can cover more ground if we split up, but then we risk losing sight of each other. If one of us gets caught, the others wouldn't know."

"We stick together," Jayde said. "Your idea might work, but what if we get stopped?"

Loch shrugged.

"Then it gets bloody," McCready said. "We'll all die, but I'm not going to live out the rest of my life in a cage."

"Me either," Loch agreed.

"Then it's settled. If there's trouble, we fight with everything we've got. Let's hope it *doesn't* come to that, though. We need to conceal our guns."

"That's going to be a problem," McCready said. "The rifles are too big. We can easily hide our pistols, but these are going to draw attention."

"Can either of you tell if that human guard is armed? If we can pass ourselves as guards, we could keep our rifles in the open."

"I don't see any weapons on him," Loch said. "I don't think we should risk it."

Jayde sighed and wondered why nothing they ever got involved with could ever be easy. After debating with herself, she handed her rifle to Loch.

"Stay here. McCready and I will go into the market. Try not to be seen. Fire off a shot if you run into trouble and we'll come running."

The look on Loch's face made it evident he didn't like the idea of being left alone. Jayde didn't give him the option of objecting. She took McCready's Silver Flux rifle and tossed it at Loch, then walked onto the main road of the city.

It was time to get things done.

6

BOTH THE CITY AND the market were a confusing maze.

Jayde and McCready got turned around several times in the city before finding the long lane that made up the market. Oddly enough, they hadn't encountered any Thraan. At least, Jayde didn't think they had. She'd never seen one and didn't know what they looked like. McCready confirmed her suspicions. He pointed out all of the alien races he recognized, and there were a few neither of them knew. There were also humans in the mix, both slaves and guards alike.

She had never seen so many different aliens mingling together in one place. The depressed and downtrodden look to them was a constant reminder that they were all slaves to the Thraan.

"I thought the Thraan killed off everyone they attacked," Jayde said to McCready. She tried to keep her voice low, but she had to speak loud enough for the soldier to hear her over the crowd.

"Sometimes they do. Most of the time, they take prisoners. The Thraan thrive on power and control. If they killed everyone they encountered, they wouldn't have anyone to lord their power over."

It was hard to wrap her mind around the fact that so many aliens had fallen victim to the Thraan. The Convocation seemed to be the only ones standing up to them, and even then, they were struggling.

"What kind of shop do you think would sell the part we need?" Jayde asked.

As if on cue, they halted directly in front of a small building that had a sign made of metal pieces that spelled out Engine Help in Gecrenish, the language of the Gecrens. They were a race of small-statured aliens that looked like oversized crickets.

"This one?" McCready said with a chuckle.

They went inside and were greeted by a large open floorplan. Tables of various sizes were scattered throughout and covered with all sorts of engine components. The prices varied anywhere from one hundred credits to one hundred thousand. Jayde exchanged glances with McCready.

"We need to figure out how to get the part out of here if they have it," she whispered.

An old Gecren hobbled out from the back of the building, his plumb body relying heavily on the small wooden cane he walked with.

"Ah, humans," he said, his alien accent almost non-existent. "What can I do for you?"

"We're looking for this," Jayde replied, holding up the holoscreen she'd taken from Loch. The image of the Erillian engine piece spun slowly around.

The Gecren eyed her warily but didn't say anything. Jayde thought the worst and was prepared to sprint out of the place when the Gecren tapped his wooden cane on the floor and the front door bolted shut.

"Why are you looking for *that*? The Thraan have proclaimed the Erillians extinct. Since they are dead, there's no need to power the ship of an Erillian."

McCready folded his arms across his chest. Jayde wasn't sure what the Gecren was hinting at, but she didn't feel that he was threatening them in any way.

"Who said it was for an Erillian ship?" Jayde asked.

"Come now," the Gecren said, his antennae curling back behind his head. "I've been working on ships longer than you've been alive. I know what I'm looking at."

"Fair enough. We need it to power an Erillian ship that we stole."

"Try again," The Gecren said. He waited patiently.

Jayde looked at McCready, but the big man just shrugged.

"Fine. Not all of the Erillians are dead," she said.

"There we go. That's what I was waiting to hear."

The Gecren shuffled over to a tall stand in the corner and rummaged through the shelves. He said something Jayde didn't understand, then turned around and brought a small box over to her. The cricket-man removed the lid and held the box out for her to see. Inside was the square part they needed, an exact replica of the image. Jayde felt a weight lift off her shoulders.

"How much?" she asked.

"Normally, the asking price is a million credits," the Gecren answered. But I'm feeling generous right now. Take me with you and you can have it."

"Take you with us where exactly?"

The old alien stared intently at Jayde. "You may have these other slaves fooled, but I know you are not slave guards. You two walk with a different bearing. I've been oppressed by the Thraan almost my entire life. I've heard the whispers. That there are those who are fighting back against the Thraan. I've suffered enough. I want to leave. I want to help. I want to fight."

Jayde felt bad for the Gecren, but how did she know she could trust him? It could be an elaborate ruse to lead the Thraan to the remaining Erillians. She could hear Loch in her mind, posing the argument that it wasn't a trap. Jayde stared at the box, then stared into the Gecren's eyes. She saw no malice, no deception. She saw hope.

"Deal," she said.

The Gecren's antennae twitched about with his excitement. He pushed the box into Jayde's hands and then retrieved a belt from the stand and hurriedly attached a number of items onto it.

"I'm ready," he announced.

"Let's get moving, then," Jayde replied.

The alien unlocked the door with a double tap of his cane on the floor, and the three of them joined the masses back in the street. It took some time to push through the crowd, but they eventually made it back to where Loch was waiting for them. He glanced at the Gecren and offered a questioning glance at Jayde.

"This is Loch," she introduced. "And this is … I'm sorry, what was your name?"

The Gecren lowered himself into a bow and said, "Lurg."

Loch still looked confused.

"I'll explain on the way," Jayde said.

A commotion broke out in the crowded streets of the city, giving Jayde a bad feeling in her stomach. Had the Thraan taken notice of them?

"We need to go," she said.

They started to leave, but she felt that leaving the human slaves behind was wrong. They deserved a choice. She took her rifle from Loch and knelt on one knee, then took aim at the cage door and fired.

The laser blast blew the lock free and the door swung open slowly. The human guard looked around in panic and tried to close the gate.

He was too late. Some of the slaves began pushing their way out of the cage, hurling themselves against the guard, knocking him down. The others followed the example and began fleeing the cage. Feeling as though she had done something good, Jayde led her crew away from the city and back to the transport tunnel.

Their suits were still where they left them, but there were signs that someone had come through the area recently. Jayde put her suit on and looked at Lurg.

"We don't have an extra suit," she said. "Can you breathe without oxygen?"

"Don't worry about me," Lurg said. He grabbed something from his belt and pressed it into his mouth.

Jayde pulled her helmet on and waited for the suit to pressurize, then she climbed the stairs and stepped into the tunnel. She couldn't explain why, but there was an urgency now. She could feel it in her blood. She kept her pace quick and led them across the bridge. When they reached the end and stepped out onto the ground of the moon, she stopped in surprise.

The largest alien she had ever seen was standing in front of the cave, lifting a crate full of crystals.

Before she could ask, McCready whispered loudly, "That's a Thraan."

It towered over eight feet in height and a trail of wicked spikes ran the length of its back. Jayde couldn't see much more of it, for it was had its back to them. They were standing in the open, and if the alien turned around, it would easily spot them. Jayde lifted her rifle and took aim. The Erillians words echoed in her mind again, telling her that nobody fought the Thraan.

Fear and common sense overruled her, and she motioned the others to follow her. She hurried to the wall of crates they had hidden behind earlier and waited. They were all breathing heavily and Jayde could already feel sweat running down her back. If the Thraan was a fast runner, it would be hard enough to outrun it with Lurg hobbling along, but even more so wearing the constricting suits. The old alien already seemed like he was going to collapse from exhaustion and they had barely run very far. Jayde risked a glance over the crates. The Thraan had disappeared.

"It must have gone into the cave," she said. "It's gone."

They left the area and traveled back to the Erillian camp. Just as before, the place seemed deserted. Knowing that the Erillians didn't intend to kill them, she walked openly into the camp and waited for the aliens to show themselves. It didn't take long before the Erillian leader to appear. She stepped out from one of the purple buildings, her two guards close at her sides.

"You have found the part we need?" she asked.

Jayde held out the box Lurg had given her and the Erillian accepted it. She looked inside and chirped to her fellows, then hand the box to one of them. He sprinted away.

"I offer you my deepest appreciation. My people will be able to escape to safety and live to fight another day."

"I'm glad that we could help," Jayde said. "However, you have something we need."

"I did not forget," the Erillian said. She pulled a thin chain out from beneath her armor. Attached to the chain was what looked like a vial, though it was made of metal instead of glass. The Erillian removed the chain from around her neck and offered it to Jayde.

Jayde accepted the vial and wrapped the chain around her hand. She looked the Erillian in the eyes and the two stared at one another in silence. They were similar, yet so different.

"Thank you," Jayde finally said.

"We have served each other mutually," the Erillian said. "May we cross paths again."

"Under better circumstances, I hope," Jayde replied. She wasn't sure, but it seemed like the alien smiled.

"Farewell, Jayde Thrin of the *Determination.*"

The Erillian and her remaining guard went back into the building, leaving Jayde and her crew alone. Jayde turned to Lurg.

"Are you sure you want to come with us?" she asked. "We're mercenaries, and our road is never smooth."

"If it means leaving behind the life of misery the Thraan forced upon me, I will go anywhere. Choosing a bumpy road is better than not being able to choose at all."

Jayde couldn't agree more. They left the Erillian camp and walked across the flat empty landscape back to the *Determination.* Klaus had turned the IDS on and she had to radio him to disable it so they could board the ship. The mechanic sounded relieved, but she knew the man would never admit it. He liked to pretend he didn't have any emotions. It was a wonder he had ever been married in the past.

As the IDS doors folded back into the ship, Jayde thought she heard a different noise. She looked back the way they had come and saw a cloud of dust rising from the ground. She took a few steps closer and squinted into the distance, but she couldn't tell what it was.

"Look," she said. "Can any of you make out what that is?"

Before Loch or McCready could answer, Lurg groaned. "It's that Thraan from the cave," he said.

"How do you know?" Jayde asked.

"We Gecrens have great eyesight," he answered. "He's coming fast."

"Everyone on the ship," Jayde ordered. "If we can't get off the ground before he reaches us, we'll turn the IDS on and he'll wear himself out trying to get through our defenses."

"No," Lurg said. "Your ship doesn't stand a chance against him."

"Then we'll stand and fight," McCready grunted.

"No," Lurg said again. "We'll all be slaughtered."

"Then what other option do we have?" Jayde asked.

"Get on the ship," Lurg said. "All of you. I'll hold him off as long as I can."

"Absolutely not," Jayde said. "We're not leaving you behind after what you've done to help us."

Lurg's antennae rubbed against one another and the old alien tossed his cane down. His back began to move oddly and before Jayde could stop him, wings burst free and Lurg flew toward the approaching Thraan.

7

"Go!" Loch shouted.

He pushed Jayde toward the ship. She was still in shock and watched Lurg's small form soar to his certain death. McCready grabbed her by the arm and pulled her as he ran for the ship. Her eyes welled with tears. She wasn't crying because Lurg was going to die; she barely knew him. She was emotional because he was sacrificing himself for them. She blinked back the tears and ran alongside McCready.

They boarded the *Determination* and Jayde ran for the observation deck. Loch followed her and McCready went below to man the laser cannons. Neither one of them spoke a word, but they quickly removed their suits and Loch threw himself into the seat at the console and prepped the ship for takeoff. Jayde placed the vial's chain around her neck.

"Are the engines ready?" Loch asked Klaus through the intercom.

"Primed and warm," Klaus answered.

Loch wasted no time. His fingers tapped at the screen wildly and before Jayde realized it, the *Determination* was in the air and soaring away from Hetania. Jayde looked down at the moon, but they were moving so quickly that she couldn't see the dust cloud anymore. A flash of light to her right caught her attention and she saw an Erillian vessel blasting away from the moon.

"We did it," she whispered.

"Incoming," Loch warned. "A Thraan battleship has targeted the Erillians."

"What?" Jayde rushed over to the console. The radar showed the Erillian vessel and another larger vessel closing in. "We've got to intercept the battleship," she said.

"What about the cure?" Loch asked.

Jayde didn't know what to do. If the Erillian vessel was destroyed, the Thraan would certainly attack the *Determination* next.

"Can we outrun the battleship?" Jayde asked.

"I doubt it," Loch replied.

"What about in hyperdrive?"

Loch hesitated. "Probably, but then we'd lead it to Earth …" he paused. "Where the *Titan* would blast the hell out of it! Nice thinking, Jayde!"

"We need to take their attention from the Erillians first."

"I've got this," Loch said.

Jayde pressed the intercom button. "McCready, get ready to light up the Thraan ship with those cannons!"

The *Determination* sped up and headed straight for the Thraan battleship. The alien vessel was crescent-shaped, with large plasma cannons mounted on the undersides of its wings.

"Shields are at a hundred percent?" Jayde asked.

"Ninety," Loch said.

"That will have to do."

The distance continued to dwindle. When they were within range, blasts from the *Determination's* cannons lit up the blackness of space and struck the side of the Thraan battleship. The vessel's shields flared as they took the brunt of the attack. The ship gave up the chase of the Erillian vessel and swung wide to face the *Determination*.

"I'd say that got their attention," Loch muttered.

"Keep us on course. We can take a direct hit or two, but then we'll need to hightail it out of here. Hopefully, the Erillians will be long gone by then."

"I'm detecting hyperdrive signatures," Loch confirmed. "The Erillians are about to be home free."

More laser cannon fire lit up the Thraan battleship, but it was doing little damage. The alien vessel fired its own cannons, striking the side of the *Determination*. The ship shuddered from the assault, but the shields held up.

"Speed up," Jayde ordered. "Take us directly over them."

Loch did as she commanded. As they passed over the top of the battleship, McCready rained cannon blasts down on the Thraan. Again, they did little damage. Jayde hoped they could wear the shields down enough to debilitate the ship, but her hopes were immediately dashed as the battleship flipped around and started blasting the back of the *Determination*. They were a decent distance past the Thraan ship, but the enemy would quickly close the gap.

"Shields are dropping quickly," Loch warned. "Seventy percent. Fifty." He looked at Jayde expectantly.

"Are the Erillians gone?"

"Yes."

"Get us back to Earth," she said.

A bright light flashed ahead of them and suddenly a Convocation Inquisitor ship appeared out of hyperspace. It began firing on the Thraan battleship with its cannons.

"I thought Logan couldn't spare any resources?" Loch asked.

"That's what he said," Jayde replied, trying to hide her smile. So, Logan had come to help her. Jayde's heart fluttered in her chest and she realized that her feelings for the man were growing more than she anticipated.

A projectile left the Inquisitor vessel and flew overhead, striking the Thraan ship a direct hit.

There was an explosion and the battleship became nothing more than metal splinters. Debris rained against the *Determination,* but the shields prevented any damage. The shockwave shook the entire ship, causing everything to rattle around them.

"Thank you, Logan," Jayde whispered. She couldn't wait to see him.

"A communication is coming from the Inquisitor," Loch said.

"Put it through."

The screen flickered on and Jayde was immediately confused. Instead of Logan, there was a young woman. She had flowing blond hair and bright blue eyes. She didn't seem tall, maybe five foot even. Jayde waved a greeting.

"Thank you for the help. Did Logan send you?"

"Who's Logan?" the woman replied. The voice was that of a young girl's, even though she looked old enough to be considered a woman.

"You're flying a Convocation ship," Jayde said slowly. "If you don't know who Logan is, then who sent you here to help us?"

"I didn't come here to help you, silly. I came here to retrieve what's mine."

"I don't understand," Jayde said.

"I'm here for *him.*"

Jayde looked at Loch. His face had gone white and he looked like he might faint.

"Who is she?" Jayde asked.

Loch opened his mouth to reply, but no words escaped his lips. He attempted to stand up but ended up collapsing onto the floor.

"Oh no!" the woman shrieked. "Is he all right?"

Jayde touched Loch's neck. He had a pulse. It was strong, too. She frowned. Had Loch passed out? That wasn't something she'd ever witnessed before. Standing, she looked back at the screen.

"He's fine. I'm sorry, who are you? And how do you know Loch?"

The woman's tone remained the same, but her lips curled into a sneer.

"I'm Isa. Lord Rasking's daughter."

Jayde's heart fell into her stomach. Lord Rasking's *daughter?* The one Loch had messed around with before they landed on M44?

"What do you mean you're here for Loch?"

"I'm here to bring him home with me," Isa replied. "And if he doesn't come with me, then I'll turn you all in for the murder of my father."

"This isn't the best place to talk about this," Jayde said. "The Thraan have a city on Dreteron. If they detect us out here, they'll kill us."

"A valid concern," Isa said. "Fine. Get some distance between your ship and the planet and let me board your ship. I'll have my soldiers follow you."

Jayde was going to argue, but Isa ended the communication. Loch groaned softly and Jayde knelt beside him and waited until his eyes fluttered open.

"What the hell is your little girlfriend doing out here following us?" she demanded.

Loch blinked several times and sat up. The color was starting to come back to his face. Jayde helped him to his feet and he looked at the screen.

"Tell me that was a vivid, horrible nightmare."

"If only," Jayde said.

"She's really here? Oh my God."

"Tell me about it. She's boarding our ship and wants to take you with her. You're going to have to convince her to leave. We're in too much danger right now for her rollercoaster of emotions."

"I'll try," Loch said. He smoothed his hair back from his face. "I told you before, *she* was all over *me*. I had nothing to do with her before that."

"I don't care about that," Jayde replied. "Get rid of her."

Loch offered his customary mock salute and Jayde left the deck. Klaus had repaired the boarding tunnel when they were on the *Titan*, so she headed there to allow Isa access to the ship once they were far from Dreteron. If Isa wanted to play out her lovestruck fantasies with Loch, it wasn't really her business, but she refused to let the petulant little girl turn them in. Besides, even if she did try to turn them in, Jayde and her crew had retrieved the cure for the Thraan disease. That had to account for something.

Once they were safety away from the Thraan outpost, Jayde waited for the Inquisitor ship to dock, occasionally glancing out the porthole. The memories of M44 threatened to overwhelm her, but she pushed them back to the edge of her mind with as much force as she could. The docking tunnel pressurized and Jayde opened the door. The door at the other end of the tunnel opened and Isa walked across the bridge to the *Determination*.

"Welcome," Jayde said. She would be civil to the girl, but the moment Isa overstayed her welcome, Jayde would get rid of the girl herself if she had to.

"Thank you," Isa replied. "Where's Loch?"

"He's piloting the ship. You know, because he's the pilot."

Isa smirked. "Take me to him?"

Jayde turned and headed for the observation deck, not bothering to see if Isa was keeping up or not. They reached the deck and Loch didn't move from his chair. Isa rushed over to stand behind him, wrapping her arms around his neck and hugging him tightly. Loch seemed hesitant to return the hug in any way. Jayde hoped he would do the right thing and get rid of the girl.

"I've missed you," Isa said. "It's felt like an eternity since you left."

It was funny, but Jayde had to agree with the girl. It had felt like an eternity since the events of M44 and their run-in with Lord Rasking.

"Tell your ship to break away so we can get out of here," Jayde said to Isa. Surprisingly, the girl did as Jayde asked and within a few minutes, the Inquisitor ship was flying behind them.

"Take us to Earth, Loch."

Loch was trying to tap buttons on the screen, but Isa's hug was hindering him.

"Why don't you sit beside me?" he told her. Isa quickly did so and rested a hand onto Loch's thigh. Jayde rolled her eyes. Loch set the course for Earth and the ship went into hyperdrive, the stars streaking before them like thin wisps of smoke. The *Determination* left Dreteron behind in the proverbial dust and Jayde clutched the vial to her chest. They were close to saving the people of Earth, close to bringing the realized hope to the Convocation.

"Jayde?" Loch's voice broke her reverie.

"Yeah?"

"The motion detectors are picking up movement on level two."

"It's probably Klaus."

"No, Klaus is in the engine room. And McCready left the gunnery bay a few minutes ago. He should be in his room by now, so I'm not sure who or what is setting off the detectors."

Jayde pursed her lips. "I'll check it out."

She sat at another console and pulled up the cameras on level two. It was darker than usual down there, but they normally kept the lights off to save power because no one was ever on that level of the ship. Jayde flipped through each camera view, seeing nothing but darkness and faint outlines of storage bins or crates.

Just as she was about to stop looking, movement on camera six caught her eye. She zoomed in and leaned forward, peering intently at the screen. Something was moving around. It was tall and thin, but the darkness obscured any details.

"I see something," Jayde said. "I'm not sure what it is, though. You don't think the Thraan from Hetania got on the ship, do you?"

"I wouldn't think so," Loch replied. "We were in the air before it would have even gotten close enough to touch the ship."

"What else could it be?" Jayde asked.

"I don't know. I can try and override the lights from here."

Jayde kept her eyes on the screen as Loch worked. She could hear Isa whispering something to him, but she couldn't make out what the girl was saying. It was probably nothing important, anyway.

"Got it," Loch said.

The lights began kicking on and the camera momentarily flickered before the screen brightened.

Jayde sucked in a breath at what the camera showed. The tall form of the Prime Minister was moving around a storage room. As all the lights came on, the Prime Minister stopped moving. A chill ran down Jayde's spine.

"What is it?" Loch asked.

"It's the Erillian Prime Minister."

The alien turned and looked at the camera, its dead eyes staring straight into Jayde's soul.

8

"HOW THE HELL IS he alive?" McCready asked, staring at the console screen.

"Technically, he's not," Loch said. "He looks like he's turned into one of those sleeper things."

"I thought the disease only affected humans?" the soldier said.

"It would make sense why the Erillians would have a cure," Jayde commented. "They might be allies with the Convocation, but why would they develop a cure unless they were being impacted by the disease themselves?"

McCready grunted. Jayde noticed he did that when he either had nothing to say or he agreed with someone. In this case, Jayde guessed it could go either way.

"Regardless, we need to deal with this before we get to Earth. I don't want to risk any of the *Titan's* crew getting infected. We can eject his body out of the ship, but we need to kill him or immobilize him somehow."

"I'll help," McCready offered.

"Thanks. Between the two of us, I think we can manage. As for you," Jayde glanced at Loch and flashed him a look, "You need to deal with what we talked about. I expect to hear good news when I'm done with the Prime Minister."

Jayde and McCready left the observation deck and headed for the elevator. The big man's presence always made her feel safer. She felt lucky that he had joined her crew, especially since he could have been paid much more with practically anyone else.

"We can't use our guns," Jayde said. "I don't want laser holes in my ship in general, and it would be *really* bad if one of us blew the entire ship to pieces while in hyperdrive."

"Agreed."

"So, how do we take him down?"

"Maybe we can find something solid to strike him in the head. Or take his legs out so he can't move much. This is going to be fun."

Jayde shook her head but a smile spread across her lips. "You're such a soldier sometimes."

"I'll take that as a compliment," McCready said with a chuckle.

"We've only got a few hours before we arrive and dock on the *Titan,* so we need to get this done quick. I'd prefer a solid plan before we get down there."

"Sometimes plans are no good," McCready said. "Sometimes you just gotta run in swinging."

"How often has that worked out for you?"

"Surprisingly, more often than planning."

Jayde shrugged. "Why not? It's one sleeper. How bad could it be?"

"Exactly," McCready said. He pushed the elevator button and the doors slid open. They stepped inside and Jayde pressed the level two button. McCready stretched his neck from side to side, popping it loudly. Jayde could never understand why he did that. It sounded painful. The elevator's descent stopped and the doors opened.

McCready peeked his head out and checked left and right, then quietly stepped out. Jayde's hands tightened into fists and she followed behind the big man, expecting the alien to come flying at them. There was only silence. The lights were all still on, for which Jayde was glad. She always had a difficult time navigating in the dark.

They walked along the hall, only pausing to check the rooms with doors that were open. Jayde doubted that sleepers had become any more sophisticated than what she'd experienced, so it was unlikely the Prime Minister would be in a room with a closed door.

A soft knocking sound drew their attention and McCready lifted a hand and put a finger to his lips. He stepped lightly and slowly moved to the doorway where the sound had come from. The soldier looked back at Jayde and nodded once.

Jayde's heart began thrumming in her chest. She was rarely afraid or nervous in situations like this, instead finding a level of exhilaration that couldn't be replicated with anything else. The only thing that made her heart beat as fast was seeing Logan. *Focus,* she told herself. *There will be time for that later.*

McCready crouched down and made his way into the room. Jayde peered inside and could see the tall outline of the Prime Minister. He was facing away from them, his arms twitching at his sides. The hood of his robes rested on his back, revealing the light green skin of the alien's head. His flesh hung loosely on his thin body. She found it odd that he looked nothing like the rest of his people.

"Stay back," McCready mouthed to her. She nodded in response and watched as the soldier sneaked across the room. As soon as he was close to the Prime Minister, he stood up to his full height and leaped onto the alien's back, wrapping his right arm around the alien's neck.

The Prime Minister immediately began thrashing around wildly. It made an unholy moaning sound and tried to pry McCready's arms away. Jayde looked around the room for something that could be used as a weapon. On one of the tables was a long piece of metal that appeared to have come loose from a crate. Jayde sprinted to the table and snatched the metal pole up, then rushed over to where McCready was struggling with the alien.

She swung the pole awkwardly, narrowly missing McCready's shoulder and grazing the Prime Minister's cheek. The alien roared angrily and tried harder to break McCready's grip. He was easily a foot and a half taller than the soldier, but

McCready was stronger than the undead alien and held on tightly.

"Crush his head or something!" the soldier shouted.

"I'm trying, but he's too damn tall!"

McCready rammed his knee into the shallow depression at the back of the alien's leg, causing the Prime Minister to drop down lower.

"Duck!" Jayde shouted as she swung with all of her strength. The metal pole struck the Prime Minister across the temple, snapping the alien's head hard to the side, breaking his neck and showering the nearby wall with black blood. Despite the powerful blow, the Prime Minister's arms still tried to break free of McCready. His head lolled uselessly, but he was very much still 'alive.'

"This one has got more fight in him than the human ones," McCready growled. He threw his weight forward and knocked the alien's body to the floor, using his own body to keep the Prime Minister pinned down.

"I can't believe he's still able to move. I practically took his head off," Jayde said. She watched the alien squirm under McCready and considered what she should do to help the soldier.

"Are you enjoying the view?" McCready asked sarcastically, grunting as he tried to keep the alien restrained.

"Sorry, I'm not sure how to help. Should I stab him in the heart or something?"

"It's worth a try."

"Roll away in three. Two. One."

McCready released the Prime Minister and rolled to the left. As soon as he was clear, Jayde lifted the pole with both hands and jabbed it down hard into the alien's back, piercing flesh and organ alike. The Prime Minister jerked a few times then lay still. Both Jayde and McCready stood breathing heavily, staring at the mutilated corpse of the Prime Minister.

"Time to dump him," Jayde said, wiping a smatter of blood from her forehead.

"Give me a second," McCready replied, stretching his right arm out and rubbing his elbow. "That was like a session in the gym. I can't imagine what it would be like fighting more than one of them."

"He was definitely more resilient than the human sleepers. I wonder if the Thraan plague affects every alien?"

"I doubt it. There are humans who are immune, so I would assume the same could be said of aliens. There's something I've been wondering," McCready said. "I suppose we should have asked the Erillian leader, but I didn't think about it then. What if we give the cure to someone who is already turned? Will it revert them back to normal?"

"That's a good question," Jayde said. "I hadn't considered it, to be honest. I was thinking that it would be given to people who had been infected before they turned. The Convocation scientists should be able to figure that out."

"I hope you're right. I'm ready now. Let's get this thing off the ship and get cleaned up."

Jayde couldn't agree more. She felt disgusting. Between the sweat and the blood, she didn't know which she disliked more. McCready grabbed the Prime Minister's arms and looked at Jayde.

"Grab his legs, will you?"

Jayde pulled the metal pole from the body and then grabbed the alien's legs and lifted. Together, they carried the corpse out of the room and down the hall to the elevator. Jayde wrinkled her nose at the odor. The corpse was a few days old and smelled like an unwashed garbage bin. She had to hold her breath to keep from gagging while the elevator took them up to the first floor.

The doors opened and they hurriedly carried the corpse to the cargo bay. There was a small chute located next to the bay doors that was just large enough to fit the Prime Minister's body through. The other side was sealed shut, so they dropped his body into the chute and then Jayde deactivated the pressure lock on the chute and the alien's body vanished into the blackness of space.

"I'm going to shower," McCready said, then left her standing in the bay by herself.

Jayde felt like they had just done something horrible, but she knew there was no reason to feel that way. The Prime Minister had died of what she assumed was the Thraan disease, so it wasn't like they murdered him. And besides that, the Erillian planet had been destroyed, so they couldn't have given him a proper burial or anything. Hell, Jayde didn't even know if the Erillians buried their dead. The curious thing was the time it took the alien to turn. Perhaps he'd had some immunity to the disease?

With a soft sigh, she left the bay and went to her personal quarters where she stripped her clothes off and took a hot shower. She washed the grime from her body and stood under the hot water, letting the warmth relax her muscles. Her eyes grew heavy. She hadn't felt so tired in such a long time.

Jayde turned the water off and got out, allowing the air dryer to dry the water from her skin. She put some clean clothes on and climbed into her bed. Loch would wake her up when they got to the *Titan,* so she allowed herself to drift off to sleep.

Her eyes snapped open and she looked around groggily. She had no idea how long she'd been out, but Loch's voice over the intercom had woken her.

"Jayde to the observation deck," the speakers crackled. "We're closing in on the *Titan.*"

Jayde forced herself to sit up and she rubbed her eyes. Despite her exhaustion, an excitement was beginning to grow in her. They were almost back to the *Titan,* back to Earth. Back to Logan. She rolled off the bed and ran a brush through her hair, checking her reflection in the mirror. Her brown locks had a few rogue curls but otherwise looked fine. She hurried to the observation deck.

Loch had a concerned look on his face. He was alone, which she found odd considering Isa couldn't leave the ship while it was in hyperdrive.

"This is Lochlan Drevil with the *Determination,* come in. We're requesting permission to dock." He looked over his shoulder at Jayde. "There's no answer from the *Titan,*" he said.

"Are we close enough for communication?" Jayde asked.

"Yes. This is the sixth time I've requested permission and there hasn't even been static on their end. What do you want me to do?"

Jayde could understand Loch's concern. There should have been someone who could respond to them. Unless something terrible had happened. Uncertainty and fear clawed at her stomach.

"Are the dock doors open?"

"Yeah. I did a scan for life forms, but the *Titan* is blocking the signal. It makes sense, considering it's a military vessel, but the doors are open."

"Get us on board and let's find out what's going on." She paused and looked at Loch. "Where's Isa?"

The brief look that passed over his face told Jayde everything she needed to know.

"She's in my quarters," he answered.

9

THE FIRST THING JAYDE noticed as she stepped out of the *Determination* was the emptiness of the hangar bay. Previously, there were easily two hundred ships with room for many more. Now, there wasn't a single vessel in sight. Nor was there a single person.

She strode across the bay towards the doorway Logan had led her through, her memory a bit hazy on the details of the route. A solitary mech caught her attention. It was in obvious disrepair with a puddle of oil around its large metal feet.

Jayde had the feeling that something terrible must have happened while they'd been gone. Had the Thraan attacked another human planet? Did some disease infected person get onto the *Titan* somehow? She could only guess as she tried to navigate her way through the various halls of the space station, searching for anyone who might be able to put her racing mind at ease. Specifically, she wanted to find Logan.

Aside from the general hum of the station, there were no other sounds. It was as if everyone had jumped ship and left the station behind. Jayde got turned around several times and was getting frustrated when she spotted something she recognized. It was the room where Logan had told her about the attack on Earth. Feeling more confident, she used the room as her starting point and retraced her steps, recalling her memory of the night she'd spent with Logan.

She found his personal quarters and barged inside, crestfallen at the lack of his presence despite the obvious signs that no one was on board the *Titan* anymore. Jayde stood there, looking around the room at what remained. Most of his personal belongings were gone which confirmed her suspicions.

Logan wasn't here.

Her next question was why? And where had he gone? She opened the drawers of his desk and his bureau. One of his uniforms had been left behind and she grabbed the sleeve of the coat and brought it to her nose, inhaling his scent. She closed her eyes and sighed. A few more deep breaths and she released the material and turned to the computer on his desk.

The system was locked and required a Convocation login. Jayde didn't bother trying to guess any credentials. What was the point? She was about to leave Logan's room when she spotted a holoscreen on the edge of the bed. Jayde grabbed it and held her finger on the button that would turn it on, but paused.

Did she really want to know what happened? With everything she and her crew had been through over the last few weeks, it seemed that bad news was the only thing she'd receive. She chose not to press the button. Not yet.

Jayde headed back to the conference room and sat down at the head of the table. She looked over the screen and pressed the button that said refreshments. The table's surface opened up and a bowl of fruit rose up from within. Jayde grabbed an apple and took a bite, relishing the sweet juice that covered her tongue. A few drops slid down her chin and she wiped them away with the sleeve of her armor.

She set the holoscreen on the table and stared at it as she devoured the apple. The desire to know what was on it was driving her crazy, but she was also afraid. Jayde reprimanded herself. She'd been in dangerous situations where she had almost died and never flinched, but she was afraid to find out where Logan was?

Pushing the fear away, she pressed the button on the holoscreen and watched as Logan's hologram face materialized. His forehead was creased in thought and he remained silent for a long moment before speaking.

"Jayde … I'm not sure if you'll ever see this or not. In the event that you are successful and come back to the *Titan,* I wanted you to know a few things."

Logan closed his eyes and tilted his head to each side, cracking his neck, then looked straight ahead. Jayde felt like he was looking directly at her, as if he wasn't just some holographic message.

"Before I get into the gritty stuff, I'm curious to know if I was *that* bad in the sack that you would disappear without saying a word to me? I mean, men have insecurities, too." He laughed. "Seriously though, I was really disappointed to wake up and find out you'd already left."

Jayde didn't regret leaving like that aside from not telling Logan goodbye. She didn't like saying those words to anyone. The universe was a dangerous place where most people in her line of work didn't enjoy longevity.

"I hope you found the cure the Erillian's claimed they had. It's definitely needed. I'm sorry I couldn't send anyone to help you, but I think you understand that I'm bound by my oath to the Convocation."

"I do understand," Jayde whispered.

Logan ran a hand through his hair and looked to the side and gave a curt nod, then turned his attention back to his recording.

"It's almost time for me to go, so I'll try to make this quick. Earth has been abandoned by the Convocation. The number of dredges down there makes trying to rescue survivors a suicide mission. We don't have the resources to spare, and even if we did, there's no telling what sort of mess we would find down there.

"Anyway, there's a small pocket of survivors that we've been in communication with. I've not told them the news that no one is coming to get them. I don't want them to give up. I know that probably sounds stupid, considering there's no way for them to get off the planet with the containment shield in place, but … it just feels wrong to steal their only hope.

"Their coordinates are 34.013071° N, -85.030200° W. We're only able to connect with them when the *Titan* is above their location. I think the shield is hindering their signal, but when it comes in clear, we have a few hours to talk with them. Their situation is getting more difficult as the days pass."

Logan paused and scratched his chin. His typical clean-shaven skin had dark splotches where the hair was growing back. Jayde studied his face, committing every detail to memory. Logan exhaled a long breath.

"The last time I spoke with them, some of their group had gotten trapped inside a building while searching for food. The dredges killed a few of them. One was a kid." Logan lowered his head. She wasn't completely certain, but Jayde thought she could see a tear sliding down his cheek.

"I wish I could help them," he said, looking back up. "But my obligations are taking me to the front lines. The Thraan are getting bolder and their forces are increasing at our borders. The Convocation has ordered the entire crew of the *Titan* to join the defenses. I've left everything behind that wasn't an immediate necessity, so feel free to take anything you need. Chances are we won't be coming back …"

Logan trailed off and looked away from the screen again. He said something Jayde couldn't make out, then he looked back at the screen.

"I know I asked a lot from you when I asked you to go to Erillia, and I wouldn't have put you in that danger if I knew you couldn't handle it. You're a tough woman, Jayde. Tougher than anyone I've met before. I'm not asking you to do anything, but I've left the override code to the containment shield in my desk. It's the second drawer on the right."

Jayde rushed to the desk drawer and opened it to find a rough hand-written note with a random sequence of numbers and letters.

"If you and your team are feeling brave, you can rescue the group of survivors on Earth. They can live on the space station for years without worrying about going hungry. There's plenty in the storage pantries. The station's power source is strong and healthy and should last at least a hundred years. Or they can find homes on other planets, though the *Titan* is probably the safest place right now. Since the Thraan have already obliterated Earth, I don't see them coming back for anything.

"The cure that the Erillians mentioned … if it does exist, we have a lab that can analyze it and generate more. I have a lot of questions about this cure, but I suppose they will have to wait. Whatever you decide to do, would you please get a message about the cure to the Convocation? We really need some hope in this bleak universe right now."

Logan moved his face closer to the screen and smiled. "I hope the universe sees fit to let us find each other again. If not, then good luck, Jayde. May you find success in everything. Goodbye."

Goodbye.

The one word she didn't want to hear, especially not from Logan. Jayde replayed the message again. A world full of sleepers with a small group of survivors? Logan was right—it was a suicide mission. Jayde considered how the Convocation had sent a ship for the survivors of Ochillon and wondered what was different now. Why did they decide to abandon Earth?

The excuse that Earth was a lost cause didn't sit well with her. It was the birthplace of humanity. How could they so easily give up? The Thraan were threatening invasion, but that didn't justify leaving innocent people to die. At the same time, what could she do? Her crew was small. Even if they agreed to help, how would they attempt to pull it off?

Jayde mulled over the dilemma as she finished her apple. She couldn't high tail it away from Earth knowing there were people stuck down there. If her crew didn't want to help, she could understand. But she had to do *something*.

She used the computer to find a map of the station and located the lab. It was a few floors down from her current position. Jayde pulled the vial out from her armor and removed the chain from her neck, then left the conference room and navigated her way to the lab. It was a large space with a blindingly white interior. The entire place was so hygienic and sterile, it made Jayde feel as though she wasn't clean enough to be there.

After twenty minutes of wandering around the lab trying to find which machine she needed, she gave up and placed the vial on a desk with a bunch of beakers. She didn't want to risk having the vial break by wearing it around. Besides, there was nobody on the ship aside from herself and her crew. It was safer here in the lab.

"Maybe Klaus can figure this out," she muttered.

Jayde left the room and went back to the hangar bay. She stopped at the mech suit and looked it over. She was certainly no mechanic, but it seemed to her that the suit could be repaired. It would be a powerful tool to use down on Earth. As if he knew she was thinking about him, Klaus appeared in the doorway of the *Determination* and departed the ship, heading in her direction.

"Have you seen this?" she asked as he neared.

"Yeah, I gave it a glance. Why?"

Jayde smiled broadly. "Can you get it up and running? I've got a task that could really use this kind of beast."

Klaus eyed her curiously but didn't ask any questions.

"I'll explain when Loch and McCready are here. Speaking of, do you know where they are?"

"They went to explore," Klaus answered. He walked behind the mech and began looking it over closely. "I don't think it will be too difficult to fix this," he said. "The work needed appears to be minor, but it'll be time-consuming.

"Good. We've got some time. As soon as the other two get back here, I'll lay out my idea."

10

As soon as the rest of the crew and Isa had rejoined Jayde and Klaus in the hangar bay, Jayde gave them the rundown of Logan's message.

"So, the Convocation is just going to leave them down there?" Loch asked. "There's no rescue coming for those people?"

"There's no rescue for those people coming from the Convocation, no."

McCready met her gaze and she could tell by the look in his eyes he knew exactly what she was planning. He moved his head slightly, a nod of understanding and support. She smiled at him in return.

"The group of survivors has been in contact with the station, but Logan didn't tell them the bad news. And I can understand why. I don't blame him. If he'd have told them, they would probably have given up trying to survive."

Loch shook his head and snorted. "They should've at least been told they've been left to die. If they want to give up, it's their choice, but they shouldn't be waiting for nothing."

"I agree with that sentiment," Jayde said. She folded her arms across her chest. "I propose we rescue them."

"Do what now?" Loch said. "How do you *propose* we fight a literal army of sleepers or dredges or whatever the hell they're called when we barely got off M44 alive?"

"Well, for one, we take that mech over there. And secondly, we take as many weapons as we can carry. Once we reach the survivors, they can help us clear a path back to the ship."

"This is suicide," Loch complained. "Seriously Jayde, this is the craziest thing you've ever suggested. We don't know if those people are even still alive."

"If you don't want to help, I get it. I'm not forcing your hand, Loch. I'm telling you that I'm going down there to offer those people a chance at life. If you want to come with me, great. If you don't, then stay here. It's fine."

"Now you're trying to guilt me," he replied, throwing his hands up in the air.

"I'm not trying to guilt you, Loch. I'm just telling you what I'm doing."

"I'll go," Isa said, surprising all of them. Loch seemed more angry than surprised, but he didn't say anything.

"I go where you go," McCready grunted. "Always have, always will."

"Thank you," Jayde said. "Klaus?"

"I'm not a fighter," the mechanic answered. "I want to help, but I don't think I'd do any of you any good down there. I'd probably end up slowing you down or getting someone killed. I'm going to stay up here and do what I can to help you once you're down there."

"Fair enough," Jayde said. She turned her gaze back on Loch. Isa also watched him.

Loch returned Jayde's stare and silence fell over the group for a long moment before he finally said, "I'm not going. I'm staying here with Klaus."

Jayde was disappointed, but she kept her emotions off her face. "That's fine with me. Would you mind helping us load some weapons from the armory into the *Determination?* I have a feeling we're going to need a lot."

He offered a nod and followed McCready out of the hangar bay. Isa followed after them and Jayde couldn't help but think of her like a lost puppy. Klaus began working on the mech and Jayde went to the kitchen. She loaded up a cart with all sorts of non-perishable foods and canisters of water, then wheeled the goods to the ship. There was no telling how long they'd be down there, and she wanted to make sure they were well stocked, especially if they managed to get the survivors on board.

She lost count of how many trips she made back and forth, but after a few hours, she stopped to take a break. Klaus had finished the repairs to the mech and McCready had jumped into the suit and walked around the hangar bay, testing the machine out. He was satisfied but mentioned that it was an older model.

"It should hold up pretty well against the dredges," the soldier said.

"That's some good news, at least," Jayde replied. "I don't know how well the two of us are going to fare down there. I wish Loch would come with us."

"I know," McCready said. "But as you said, you can't force his hand. He's a grown man and has to make the decision for himself."

Jayde knew the man was right, but it didn't make her feel any better. Four people with guns were better than three. Once the mech was loaded into the cargo bay of the *Determination*, the crew put together a large meal and ate well, sharing stories from their pasts as they sat around the communication console waiting to hear from the survivors on Earth. The coordinates Logan had given Jayde were slowly getting closer.

"What's on the schedule after this?" Loch asked during a lull in the conversation.

"What do you mean?" Jayde said.

"After this rescue mission, what's next on the agenda for us? Any ideas for our next job?"

Jayde considered the question internally. She honestly hadn't thought about it. She'd expected to come back and hand the cure off to Logan, possibly bed him again and then … she didn't know. She'd toyed with the idea of staying with Logan, but realized that wouldn't be possible unless she joined the Convocation or married Logan. Neither of those scenarios excited her. She liked Logan a lot, but she wasn't ready for marriage. She'd never been tied down before, and she still had the vastness of the universe to see.

"I don't know," she answered. "I was thinking we could wing it. Pick a random planet and see what happens."

"That sounds kind of fun," Loch said with a smile. "No imminent death, not being stranded in deep space … I wouldn't know how to act."

Everyone laughed, including Jayde. "I know, right?" she said. "We haven't had the best luck, that's for sure. But I think our cards are about to change. I can feel it. The winds of change are going to blow the *Determination* just where she needs to be."

"You're coming back with me after this, aren't you?" Isa asked Loch.

The comms erupted with static, interrupting their conversation and causing everyone to startle.

"This is Stefan with the Remnant, come in Titan."

Jayde looked around at each of her crew and slowly rose to her feet and walked to the console. She tapped the screen and moved the satellites on the station to make the signal stronger.

"Remnant, this is Jayde Thrin of the *Determination.* What's your status?"

"Jayde? You're a new voice. Where's Logan?"

"Logan's been … reassigned," Jayde said. "I'm taking over the rescue mission."

"What did you say? You broke up for a second. Did you say rescue?"

Jayde steeled herself, wanting to sound confident despite the fact that she felt like she had no idea what she was about to do.

"Correct. We're coming to get you, Remnant."

There was a brief silence, but when Stefan spoke again it sounded like there was a celebration happening among the others with him. He told them to quiet down.

"That's great news, Titan. You've just boosted the morale down here. We were starting to get worried when we didn't hear from you yesterday."

"We were having some difficulties, but we're back on track now. We're planning to land on Earth this time tomorrow, assuming everything goes to plan. Is there anything we need to know? A good spot to land, free of buildings and light on the sleepers?"

"Sleepers? Do you mean dredges?"

"Yes."

"There's an old shopping center with a decent sized parking lot that you should be able to land on. It's a mile or so from our current location, but it's the closest you'll be able to get for a safe landing."

"That'll have to work. How many of you are there?"

Jayde was hoping to have enough room on the ship for everyone, but if they had a few hundred people, it would require two trips. She was surprised when Stefan answered and said, "There's about twenty of us left."

She was stunned. Only twenty? That wasn't many people at all. It was still worth the effort of a rescue mission, but she expected a few hundred at a minimum.

"The Thraan must have really devastated Earth," Jayde whispered to herself. "Any children?" she asked.

"One. A girl. She's my daughter."

"That's good. How old is she?"

"She's six." The little girl's voice chimed in the background, saying, "I'm six and a half!"

Jayde laughed. Despite what the people were going through, the child still had a way of making them laugh. The commotion died down and Stefan lowered his voice.

"Tell it to me straight," he said quietly. "How likely is it that you'll actually reach us?"

"I'll fight demons from hell to reach you. How's that?"

"Thank you, Jayde. That's reassuring. I believe you. Be careful when you get here. The dredges are everywhere. You just might get your chance."

"My chance for what?" Jayde asked.

"Your chance to fight demons. That's what they look like, the dredges."

The terrible memory of Gavin's twisted undead face snarling at her flashed in her mind. She didn't think that dark image would ever leave her.

"We're ready for them," Jayde said. "I'll have a man here on the station in contact with you when the rest of us descend to Earth. He should be able to communicate with us as well, so if anything comes up, let him know and he can get the info to us."

"I will. Our signal is breaking up, Jayde. Until tomorrow.

"Until tomorrow," Jayde repeated. The signal from Earth terminated and Jayde turned to look at her crew.

"Tomorrow we fly. Tomorrow we fight."

ABOUT THE AUTHOR

Richard Fierce is a fantasy and space opera author. He's been writing since childhood, but began publishing in 2007. Since then, he's written multiple novels and short stories.

In 2000, Richard won Poet of the Year for his poem *The Darkness*. He's also one of the creative brains behind the Allatoona Book Festival, a literary event in Acworth, Georgia.

A recovering retail worker, he now works in the tech industry when he's not busy writing.

He's married and has three step-daughters (pray for him), three dogs (huskies!), a cat, and two ferrets. He basically has a zoo.

His love affair with fantasy was born in high school when a friend's mother gave him a copy of *Dragons of Spring Dawning* by Margaret Weis and Tracy Hickman.